Our First Day of School

An Evan and Cassie Adventure

Other books by Beth Smith

Coming Soon!
Magical Tree House

Our First Day of School

An Evan and Cassie Adventure

B. M. Smith

SPEAKING VOLUMES, LLC
NAPLES, FLORIDA
2021

Our First Day of School

Copyright © 2021 by Beth Smith

Illustrations by Rebekah Lauzier

ISBN 978-1-64540-583-2

To all the teachers everywhere.

OUR FIRST DAY OF SCHOOL

Summer had come to an end. The summer activities like swimming at the community center were gone. They had been replaced with fall activities like carving pumpkins, raking leaves, and roasting marshmallows.

Evan and Cassie awoke this morning feeling excited, happy and a little nervous. This exciting day has arrived, the new clothes and the new backpack will be worn today. Enjoying a quick breakfast while heading out the door for school.

When Mom walks Evan and Cassie to their classroom, they saw all the children getting off the big yellow bus while others were crying.

This is Evan's first year of school. He is in Pre-k and his sister Cassie in Kindergarten.

Cassie is already enjoying school while skipping next to her Mom down the large hall way, singing her song…

"I love my first day, I love my first day of school."
Evan heard Cassie sing. He smiles then joined his
sister in singing the tune. "I love my first day, I love
my first day of school."

Mom and Evan walk Cassie to her classroom. Where Cassie had friends she remembered from last year, come up and talk to her. She didn't feel so all alone.

Cassie gave Mom a big hug.

Down the hallway, was Evan's classroom. Evan walks in, looking at all the toys on the shelf and the color boards on the wall. His attention is now in the corner looking and playing with the colorful wooden trains.

This made him feel at home.

"Bye Evan, I will see you later." Evan ran over to give his Mom a big hug, then he went back to the colorful wooden trains.

Evan loves the colorful wooden trains. He plays there until it was time to settle into their seats.

Coming in from recess, Evan and his class marched down to the cafeteria for lunch, where the smells of the fresh baked pizza and french fries became so appealing. The trays of food look so delicious and good.

A metal counter stretch across the room. Where they
had a variety of food from corn dogs, hamburgers, and
pizza, of course, Evan chose his favorite.

Evan sat eating his lunch with his classmates, when he saw his sister standing in line for her lunch. He smiles big. Cassie then waves.

Evan sat in his class watching a number video. The vividness of the colors with the numbers made it so easy for Evan to learn his numbers.

As Mom stands in the classroom doorway, Evan says
to Mom, "It wasn't that bad!" He then ran across the
room hugs her. "I played on the monkey bars outside
and I have a new best friend!"

Evan said while jumping up and down next to Mom."I had my favorite food for lunch and I even saw Cassie getting her lunch."

Evan standing next to Mom while tugging on her shirt. "They had all kinds of fun games, I played with and fun things I did. I had so much fun playing duck, duck, goose outside."

"My first day of school and I love it!" Evan running
around the room, with his arms extended out like an
airplane.

Evan walking out of the classroom singing…

"I love my First Day, I Love my First Day of School."

On Sale Now!

L. SYDNEY ABEL
CHILDREN FANTASY BOOKS

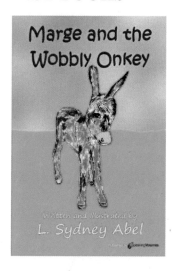

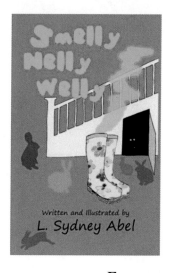

Made in the USA
Monee, IL
13 June 2022